Give that back, Jack!

A cautionary tale

Phil Roxbee Cox

Illustrated by Jan McCafferty

Edited by Jenny Tyler
Designed by Non Figg

This is the story of Jack...

...who took things
and never gave them back.

When Jack was a baby,
he snatched another baby's rattle.

And everyone said...

"Give that back,
Jack!"

When Jack was a toddler,
he took other toddlers' toys.

And everyone said...

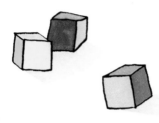

"Give them back,
Jack!"

When Jack started school,
he stole a pencil from Penny's pocket.

8

And everyone said...

"Give that back, Jack!"

What Jack wanted, Jack took...

...cakes...

...drinks...

...money...

...toys.

And everyone said,

"Give them back,
Jack!"

"They're not yours."

One day, Jack's class
goes to the zoo.
On the bus, Jack takes Ben's book.

At the zoo, he grabs a banana
from the gorilla's cage.

Then, he steals a fish
from the penguin pool.

14

And everyone says...

"Give them back, Jack!"

"They're not yours."

Now, Jack wants the ball in the sleeping lion's paws.

And everyone screams...

"Aghh!"

But Jack runs away to the Reptile House.

There he spots Mac the Python.

...where there's
NO ONE
to say...

"Give him back, Jack!
He's not yours!"

When it's time
to go home,
Jack is nowhere
to be seen.

Then Ben gasps
and points.

And everyone says...

"Give Jack back, Mac!"

But it is too late.